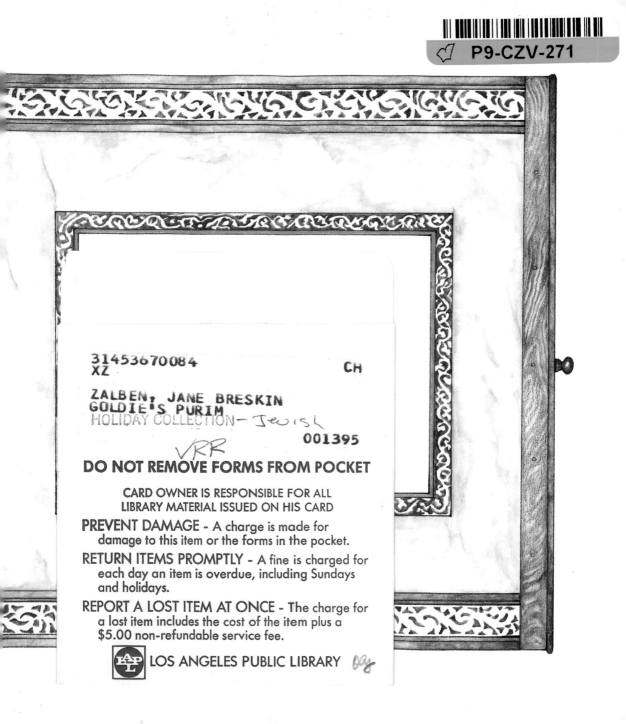

Goldie's Purim

Goldie's Purim

· STORY AND PICTURES BY ·
JANE BRESKIN ZALBEN

שִׂמְחַת פּוּרִים

HENRY HOLT AND COMPANY | *New York*

Library of Congress Cataloging-in-Publication Data
Zalben, Jane Breskin.   Goldie's Purim / story and pictures by Jane Breskin Zalben.
Summary: Although Goldie is scared at first, she overcomes her stage
fright to play Queen Esther in the synagogue's celebration of Purim.
ISBN 0-8050-1227-3
[1. Purim—Fiction.   2. Plays—Fiction.   3. Jews—Fiction.]   I. Title.
PZ7.Z254Go   1991   [E]—dc20   90-43153

Henry Holt books are available at special discounts
for bulk purchases for sales promotions, premiums,
fund-raising, or educational use. Special editions or
book excerpts can also be created to specification.
Printed in the United States of America on acid-free paper. ∞
First edition   •   Typography by Jane Breskin Zalben
1   3   5   7   9   10   8   6   4   2

To my brother,
who originally said "Go, Vashti!"
and to my children,
who have made Purim come alive again

Good smells of *hamantaschen* baking filled every corner of the house. Mama and Papa cut the flat pastry into circles, spreading poppy seeds, thick prune butter, and sweet apricot preserves in each center. Goldie, her sister, Molly, and her brother, Sam, sewed their costumes for the Purim play the following day.

They practiced their lines while they went around the neighborhood giving *shalach manot*— little gifts of food—to their family and friends.

At bedtime Goldie put the finishing touches on her dress. She laid her crown and veil on the rocker. Mama gave her a big good-night hug. "You'll be wonderful tomorrow as Esther." Goldie closed her eyes, dreaming of her special part.

The next morning every seat in the synagogue was filled. Goldie saw her grandparents, aunts, uncles, and little cousins. Her best friends, Leo and Blossom, waved.

Goldie was too scared to wave back.

First Goldie heard her sister, Molly,
who was the beautiful Queen Vashti.
"Even though the king has called
for me, I will not go and see him!"

Then Goldie heard her cousin Beni,
who played the King, Ahasuerus.
"Vashti is no longer the Queen!
Search the kingdom for a new wife."

Sam, who had the part of Mordecai, said, "I will bring my cousin Esther to the palace." Now Goldie knew it was her turn. Everyone looked at Goldie. Her legs trembled. She didn't move. She didn't speak. Sam shouted,

"Go, Esther!" Goldie thought about how brave Esther was, and how she'd have to be brave too. Goldie stepped forward and said all her lines perfectly. At the end of the play, the longest and loudest applause was for Goldie.

Then Papa took out the *megillah*. He opened the scroll and read the story of Esther, who became Queen of Persia and saved the Jewish people from wicked Haman. Every time the name of Haman was spoken, the children whirled their *groggers* in the air and stamped their feet, making a lot of noise.

They paraded around the temple in their costumes with all the parents, danced and sang, saw a puppet show, and ate a special dinner.

Everybody ate the *hamantaschen* that Goldie's family had baked. Poppy seeds got stuck between their teeth.

That night Goldie looked outside her
bedroom window at the winter moon.
The last patches of snow had already
begun to melt. Spring was on its way.
Goldie heard Sam snoring in his room,
rumbling like a *grogger*. She giggled.
Mama tiptoed in. "I'm very proud of you."
Goldie looked up. "I was scared, Mama."
"But you stopped being scared. Every person
can be brave if she tries." And she kissed Goldie.
"Like Esther was with the King!" said Goldie.
Then she smiled. "And like I was today."

PURIM PLAY (Spiel)
Cast of Characters

King Ahasuerus (*Beni*)   Ruler of the vast Persian Empire.

Queen Vashti (*Molly*)   Favorite wife of King Ahasuerus until he banished her for disobeying his commands.

Esther (*Goldie*)   A beautiful young Jewish woman chosen by Ahasuerus to be his new Queen. Through the bravery of Esther the Jewish people were saved.

Mordecai (*Sam*)   Esther's cousin, who warned the King of a plot against his life by Bigthan and Teresh, members of the court. He became a trusted advisor to Ahasuerus after Haman's death.

Haman (*Max*)   The chief advisor to King Ahasuerus. Haman hated Mordecai because Mordecai refused to bow down to him. Haman cast lots (*purim*) to determine the day on which the Jewish people would be destroyed. Haman's evil plot to kill all the Jews of Persia was stopped when Esther told the King of Haman's plan.

Hamantaschen, named after the wicked Haman, are triangle-shaped pastries eaten on the joyful holiday of Purim. Some people think that Haman wore a three-cornered hat. Others say that he had pointy ears that looked like triangles. These pastries are also known as "Haman's pockets" because in Yiddish *tashn* means "pockets." Hamantaschen, along with fruits and nuts, are given out in gift packages (*shalach manot*) to friends, as Mordecai instructed all Jews to do on the first Purim celebration.

HAMANTASCHEN

3 cups flour
1/2 tsp. baking soda
2 tsps. baking powder
1/4 tsp. salt
2/3 cup sugar
1/8 tsp. cinnamon

1/4 cup cream cheese
1/2 cup margarine
1/2 tsp. vanilla
2 tbsps. milk
2 tbsps. orange juice
1 egg

filling (see below)

1. Sift flour, baking soda, and baking powder.
   Then mix in salt, sugar, and cinnamon. Set aside.
2. Cream together softened cream cheese and margarine.
3. Add vanilla, milk, orange juice, and egg to creamed mixture,
   blending well.
4. To form a soft dough, add dry ingredients to creamed
   ingredients in a food processor or mixer.
5. Place dough onto a lightly floured board or table and roll
   out with rolling pin until dough is about 1/8″ thick.
6. Cut into 2″ circles using an upside-down glass.
7. Fill each circle with 1/2 tsp. of filling, which can be
   poppy seeds, prune or apple butter, apricot preserves,
   pitted cherries, chocolate chips, or minced walnuts and honey.
8. Press three sides of the circle together and pinch to make
   triangles. Place hamantaschen on a greased cookie sheet.
9. Bake 10 minutes or until golden brown in a preheated 350° oven.

*Note: This is a dairy recipe. If pareve, substitute water
for milk, and additional margarine for cream cheese.*